THE LAND BEYOND THE WALL

by **Veronika Martenova**
Charles

NIMBUS
PUBLISHING LTD.
— NIMBUS.CA —

Nimbus Publishing Limited
3660 Strawberry Hill St, Halifax, NS B3K 5A9
(902) 455-4286 nimbus.ca

Printed and bound in Canada
NB1497

Design: Heather Bryan
Editor: Whitney Moran

Library and Archives Canada Cataloguing in Publication

Title: The land beyond the wall : an immigration story /
[written and illustrated by] Veronika Martenova Charles.
Names: Charles, Veronika Martenova, author, illustrator.
Description: Reprint. Originally published: Halifax, Nova Scotia: Nimbus Publishing, 2017.
Identifiers: Canadiana 20190152516 | ISBN 9781771087797 (softcover)
Classification: LCC PS8555.H42242 L36 2019 | DDC jC813/.54—dc23

Nimbus Publishing acknowledges the financial support for its publishing activities from the Government of Canada, the Canada Council for the Arts, and from the Province of Nova Scotia. We are pleased to work in partnership with the Province of Nova Scotia to develop and promote our creative industries for the benefit of all Nova Scotians.

ONCE, the world was divided by a *BIG* wall.
On one side the sun rarely shone.
Fields lay bare, towns and villages were grey,
and shops were empty. People spoke in whispers
because they were afraid of each other.
They could not even trust their friends.

NOBODY WAS ALLOWED OUTSIDE THE WALL.

This was where Emma lived.

One day when Emma came home from school,
she found her parents in the garden.
They were listening to the crackling voices
from the other side of the wall.

"Don't tell anyone about this," they warned Emma.
"Listening to the voices from the outside is *FORBIDDEN*.
We could be punished if someone told on us," they said.

They didn't notice that the window was open. They didn't
know their neighbour was listening, and went to tell on them.

When Emma came home the next day,
her parents were not there.
Instead, two men were waiting inside.

"Your parents will not be coming back,"
the men told Emma.
"We're sending you to live with your aunt."

So Emma came to live with her aunt
in a small town by the sea.

Just like the land withered from lack of
sunshine, Aunt Lily was broken by the life
she led.

Her heart had shrivelled and become numb.

To her, Emma was just an extra
mouth to feed.

"*YOU MUST EARN YOUR KEEP*," she told Emma,
and she gave her chores to do in the house
and yard.

All day long Emma worked hard to
please her, but still her aunt barely
spoke to her.

Emma was lonely and missed her parents.

One day, when her chores were finished,
Emma found a pencil and paper
and took them outside to draw.

She felt comforted, almost happy,
as the pencil glided over the paper
and the shapes of trees and plants
began to appear.
Yes, she was alone, but when she drew
she wasn't lonely anymore.

When I grow up, she dreamed,
I want to be an artist.
Then I will paint the sky blue and flowers
in all colours of the rainbow.

It wasn't long before Aunt Lily caught Emma drawing.

"*PUT THAT DOWN!* Stop wasting your time and do something useful!" she scolded.

"But I want to be an artist. I have to practice so I can go to art school," Emma replied.

"Don't even think about it," Aunt Lily said.
"No school will take you after what your parents did.
Now go and sweep up the floor in the attic.
If I catch you drawing again, you'll go to sleep without supper."

Emma swept as her tears fell to the attic floor.

Suddenly, her eyes caught something in the corner.
It was an old doll.

She picked her up.

"I'm so unhappy," Emma told the doll. "I want to be an artist but I'm not allowed to draw. And I'm lonely. I have no friends to talk to."

The doll stared back. *You can talk to me*, she said.

Emma was amazed.

"You can speak?" she asked.

I used to belong to your mother, said the doll. *I can keep you company.*

Emma hugged the doll close. "I would like that," she said.

From then on, the doll was her constant companion.

One morning at dawn, Emma looked through the window.

A big sailboat was gliding into the harbour. It was not like any Emma had ever seen. Its wood was the colour of honey and its sails were fine like wisps of clouds.

"I wonder where the boat is coming from," Emma said to her doll.

You should go and find out, came the doll's answer.

So, while Aunt Lily slept, Emma tucked the doll into her pocket and snuck down to the harbour.

    The captain of the boat wore different clothes than the townspeople.

    "Good morning!" Emma said to him. "Where are you coming from?"

    "I've sailed from the other side of the ocean," the captain replied. "I'm making a stop here and then going back."

    "What is it like on the other side?" Emma asked.

    "There is a land where dreams come true."

    "Could I become an artist in that land?" Emma wanted to know.

"People there are free to be whatever they want," the captain said.

"Please, can you take me with you?" asked Emma.

"My dear child," the captain replied, "I can take you, but you will lose your voice on the other side. That's the price you will have to pay."

"Will I ever speak again?" Emma asked.

The captain smiled. "That depends on you," he said. "But you should know something else. If you leave, you can NEVER come back here."

Emma squeezed the doll in her pocket, wondering what she should do.

Go and take the chance, the doll whispered.

"I will come along with you," Emma told the captain. Her heart pounding, Emma climbed aboard.

She watched the sails fill with wind and felt the boat move.

The shore grew distant until it became just a sliver on the horizon. Then there was just the sea and the sky.

What if I've made a mistake? What if I never speak again? Emma worried. She caressed the doll and held her tight.

Have faith in yourself, a voice told her.

Help comes to those who dare.

Night fell and the wind picked up. A storm was brewing.

The boat tossed around as waves crashed against it and poured over its deck.

Emma helped the captain bail water out of the boat. She was drenched, frightened, and seasick. Only after the storm blew away was Emma able to rest.

Days stretched into weeks. And weeks stretched into months. Emma began to wonder if they would ever arrive. Finally, one day she saw a lighthouse on the horizon. This must be the land on the other side of the ocean, she thought. This will be my new home.

When Emma stepped onto dry land it was cold, and she shivered in her light summer dress. People came out of a big wooden building to take her inside.

"Don't be afraid," the captain called.
"You will have to stay in this place for a while, but you are safe. I'll come to see you in a few days."

Emma was taken inside the building and led upstairs through a maze of corridors and halls to a large room filled with metal beds. A few other grey people wandered through the hallways. They, too, seemed to have lost their voices.

Those must be people like me, thought Emma.
They must have come from the land beyond the wall.

Alone that night, and feeling lost in a large room, Emma was hungry and scared.

"What have I done?" she cried.

I'm here, came the doll's voice. *I won't leave you.*
Look out the window across the hall. It will keep your spirits up.

Through the window, Emma saw the ocean. A white lighthouse with its warm light was flickering in the night.

In a few days the captain returned with a kind-looking woman. "This lady will help you," he told Emma. "She knows you can't speak. I wish you good luck."

THOSE WERE THE LAST WORDS EMMA UNDERSTOOD.

The lady took Emma's hand and they left the building. As they walked through the city, Emma saw a strange new world, full of colours and things she had never seen before.

They stopped along the way and the lady picked up some warm clothes for Emma to wear.

Then she brought her to a house where there were other girls too. In the evening, Emma was fed dinner and given a soft bed to sleep in.

Around her, the other girls talked to each other, but the sounds had no meaning to Emma.

HOW WILL I EVER FEEL AT HOME IF I CAN'T UNDERSTAND ANYONE? she wondered.

Be patient, the doll told her. *You still have your eyes. Observe everything around you and speak with your drawings. Listen and watch. In time you will begin to understand.*

The next day, Emma found a shed with gardening tools.
For weeks, she took care of the garden near the house.
Sometimes, when her work was done, she practiced drawing pictures in the soft earth with a broken stick.

Emma didn't think that anyone would notice.

One summer morning when Emma came down
for breakfast, there was a box of paints at her
place on the table.

She looked at the lady, who smiled and nodded.
The paintbox was a gift. Now, Emma could
practice to become a real artist.

Emma smiled back at the lady, picked up her
paints, put her doll in her pocket, and hurried outside.

She walked through the city until she came to
a big park.

Flowers of every colour bloomed in the gardens,
and Emma painted them all:
dabs of yellow and orange for the marigolds,
pink and red for the roses,
purple and mauve for the lupins.

THEN SHE PAINTED THE SKY THE BLUEST OF BLUES.

A little boy and his mother came by to look at Emma's painting. The boy pointed at the picture and said something.

What Emma heard took her breath away.

The sounds had meaning!

They were words, and Emma understood them!

"That's a beautiful picture," the boy said.

Emma opened her mouth. "Here, take it," she heard herself say as she handed the boy the picture. "It's yours now. I can make another one."

I CAN UNDERSTAND! I CAN SPEAK AGAIN! Emma realized.

"Thank you," said the boy. "I will keep it forever."

He waved as he and his mother walked away.

Emma pulled out her doll.

"Did you hear?" she asked. "I can speak those sounds!
The boy understood me! That changes everything.
I'm beginning to feel that this land is my home."

But this time there was no answer.
The doll gazed back silently at Emma. Her work was done.

Emma kissed the doll's little face.

"Thank you for being with me when I needed you."

It was time to let go. From now on, Emma could take care of
herself. She could make it on her own.

When Emma was back in her room,
she wrapped the little doll carefully in paper
and laid her gently in a shoebox.
Perhaps she would keep it for her own children.

Then she sat down and wrote a letter.

Dear Aunt Lily,

I hope you are doing well.
I want to tell you that I am
following your advice —
I am being useful.
Today, I made a little boy
happy with my drawing.

Yours truly,
Emma

Emma continued to draw.

One day, she did indeed become an artist.

She now spends her time in a world of colour,
painting pictures and writing stories
for children's books.

It makes the children happy and it makes her happy too.

AFTERWORD

AFTER the end of the Second World War, Europe was divided into two separate areas: the Eastern and Western Blocs. The dividing boundary became known as the Iron Curtain.

The citizens of the Eastern Bloc countries were not allowed any contact with the Western Bloc and were not permitted to travel anywhere past the Iron Curtain. After 1950, emigration from east to west was not possible. To prevent any escape attempts, double fences of barbed wire with guard towers were placed along this dividing border and were patrolled with armed guards.

Like Emma, I was born behind the Iron Curtain, in the Eastern, Soviet-controlled Bloc. Just like Emma, I dreamt of becoming an artist, but my grandmother stopped me from attending art classes because she thought drawing was a waste of time. In an act of rebellion, I turned to music and became a rock singer. Success soon followed, and I became a member of an elite group of entertainers who were, on occasion, permitted to travel abroad to perform. Still, there were always agency officials who travelled along and closely watched our every move.

On the way home from one of our performances abroad—a concert tour of Cuba—I made a decision that altered my life's course. When the Cuban plane I was travelling on briefly stopped to refuel at Gander, Newfoundland, I decided to defect and stay in Canada. I would start my life over again and study art the way I had dreamed of when I was a child.

Like Emma, I, too, was alone, had no possessions, and no knowledge of the English language. I had lost my voice but gained hope to fulfill my ambition. Immediately, the immigration officers transported me to Halifax and placed me in detention quarters at Pier 21.

It was 1970 and Pier 21 was in its last phase of existence. The big ships carrying immigrants were no longer coming, as most were now arriving by air. At that time Pier 21 served mainly as a holding facility for political defectors from the Soviet Bloc. The two last groups of immigrants that were housed there were Cubans, who landed in Gander and waited for the political asylum, and Czech refugees who fled their country in 1968. So, in a strange way, my own story, a Czech arriving from Cuba, seems to represent the end of the era of Pier 21 acting as an immigration building.

I waited for three months in Pier 21 until I was issued a temporary permit, which allowed me to stay and work in Canada. What helped the most during this difficult time was the kindness and compassion shown to me by the volunteers, particularly Sister Florence Kelly from the Sisters of Service (who is the lady in the story taking care of Emma), and Reverend J. P. C. Fraser and his wife. I will never forget them.

The Iron Curtain was finally officially dismantled in 1990, after the fall of the Berlin Wall. All this is now history. But kindness and compassion, the human traits that help us all in times of need, remain.